'INTENSE SEXUAL DESIRE IS THE GREATEST THING IN THE WORLD.'

KATHY ACKER
Born 1947, Manhattan, New York, USA
Died 1997, Tijuana, Mexico

First published in 1981.

KATHY ACKER IN PENGUIN MODERN CLASSICS
Blood and Guts in High School
Great Expectations (forthcoming)

KATHY ACKER

New York City in 1979

Photographs by Anne Turyn

PENGUIN BOOKS

PENGUIN CLASSICS

UK | USA | Canada | Ireland | Australia
India | New Zealand | South Africa

Penguin Books is part of the Penguin Random House group
of companies whose addresses can be found at
global.penguinrandomhouse.com.

This edition first published 2018
007

Photos © 1981 Anne Turyn, originally published in Top Stories #9:
N.Y.C. in 1979 by Kathy Acker. (Top Stories was a chapbook series
featuring one author per volume. www.topstoriesperiodical.com)
Text © 1981 Kathy Acker, from Hannibal Lecter, My Father,
Semiotext(e), 2007. Reproduced with kind permission of Semiotext(e)

Set in 12/15 pt Dante MT Std
Typeset by Jouve (UK), Milton Keynes
Printed and bound in Great Britain by Clays Ltd, Elcograf S.p.A.

ISBN: 978–0–241–33889–6

www.greenpenguin.co.uk

to Jeanne's insulted beauty

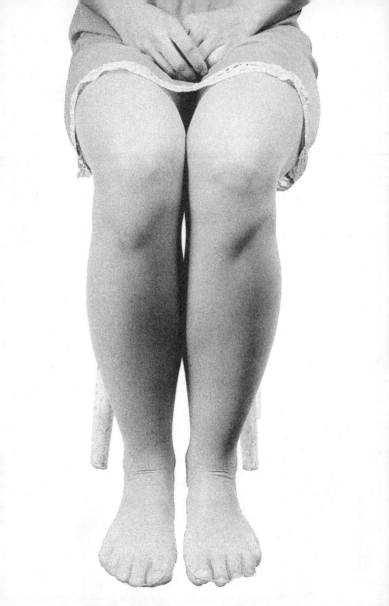

SOME people say New York City is evil and they wouldn't live there for all the money in the world.

These are the same people who elected Johnson, Nixon, Carter President and Koch Mayor of New York.

The Whores In Jail At Night

- Well, my man's gonna get me out of here as soon as he can.
- When's that gonna be, honey?
- So what? Your man pays so he can put you back on the street as soon as possible.
- Well, what if he wants me back on the street? That's where I belong. I make him good money, don't I? He knows that I'm a good girl.
- Your man ain't anything! Johnny says that if I don't work my ass off for him, he's not going to let me back in the house.
- I have to earn two hundred before I can go back.

- Two hundred? That ain't shit! You can earn two hundred in less than a night. I have to earn four hundred or I might just as well forget sleeping, and there's no running away from Him. My baby is the toughest there is.
- Well, shit girl, if I don't come back with eight hundred I get my ass whupped off.
- That's cause you're junk.
- I ain't no stiff! All of you are junkies. I know what you do!
- What's the matter, honey?
- You've been sitting on that thing for an hour.
- The pains are getting bad. OOgh. I've been bleeding two days now.
- OOgh OOgh OOgh.
- She's gonna bang her head off. She needs a shot.
- Tie a sweater around her head. She's gonna break her head open.
- You should see a doctor, honey.
- The doctor told me I'm having an abortion.
- Matron. Goddamnit. Get your ass over here matron!

- I haven't been bleeding this bad. Maybe this is the
  real abortion.
- Matron! This little girl is having an abortion!
  You do something. Where the hell is that asshole
  woman? (The matron throws an open piece of
  Kotex to the girl.) The service here is getting
  worse and worse!
- You're not in a hotel, honey.
- It used to be better than this. There's not even
  any goddamn food. This place is definitely going
  downhill.
- Oh, shutup. I'm trying to sleep. I need my sleep,
  unlike you girls, cause I'm going back to work
  tomorrow.
- Now what the hell do you need sleep for? This is
  a party. You sleep on your job.
- I sure know this is the only time I get any
  rest. Tomorrow it's back on the street again.
- If we're lucky.

LESBIANS are women who prefer their own ways to male ways.

LESBIANS prefer the convoluting halls of sensuality to direct goal-pursuing mores.

LESBIANS have made a small world deep within and separated from the world. What has usually been called the world is the male world.

Convoluting halls of sensuality lead to depend on illusions. Lies and silence are realer than truth.

Either you're in love with someone or you're not. The one thing about being in love with someone is you know you're in love: You're either flying or you're about to kill yourself.

I don't know anyone I'm in love with or I don't know if I'm in love. I have all these memories. I remember that as soon as I've gotten fucked, like a dog I no longer care about the man who just fucked me who I was madly in love with.

So why should I spend a hundred dollars to fly to Toronto to get laid by someone I don't know if I love I don't know if I can love I'm an abortion? I mean a hundred dollars and once I get laid I'll be in agony: I won't be doing exactly what I want.

I can't live normally i.e. with love so: there is no more life.

The world is gray afterbirth. Fake. All of New York City is fake is going to go all my friends are going crazy all my friends know they're going crazy disaster is the only thing that's happening.

Suddenly these outbursts in the fake, cause they're so open, spawn a new growth. I'm waiting to see this growth.

I want more and more horrible disaster in New York cause I desperately want to see that new thing that is going to happen this year.

JANEY is a woman who has sexually hurt and been sexually hurt so much she's now frigid.

She doesn't want to see her husband anymore. There's nothing between them.

Her husband agrees with her that there's nothing more between them.

But there's no such thing as nothingness. Not here. Only death whatever that is is nothing. All the ways people are talking to her now mean nothing. She doesn't want to speak words that are meaningless.

Janey doesn't want to see her husband again.

The quality of life in this city stinks. Is almost nothing. Most people now are deaf-mutes only inside they're screaming. BLOOD. A lot of blood inside is going to fall. MORE and MORE because inside is outside.

New York City will become alive again when the people begin to speak to each other again not information but real emotion. A grave is spreading its legs and BEGGING FOR LOVE.

Robert, Janey's husband, is almost a zombie.

He walks talks plays his saxaphone pays for groceries almost like every other human. There's no past. The last six years didn't exist. Janey hates him. He made her a hole. He blasted into her. He has no feeling. The light blue eyes he gave her; the gentle hands; the adoration: AREN'T. NO CRIME. NO BLOOD. THE NEW CITY. Like in Fritz Lang's METROPOLIS.

This year suffering has so blasted all feelings out of her she's become a person. Janey believes it's necessary to blast open her mind constantly and destroy

EVERY PARTICLE OF MEMORY THAT SHE
LIKES.

A sleeveless black T-shirt binds Janey's breasts.
Pleated black fake-leather pants hide her cockless-
ness. A thin leopard tie winds around her neck. One
gold-plated watch, the only remembrance of the
dead mother, binds one wrist. A thin black leather
band binds the other. The head is almost shaved.
Two round prescription mirrors mask the eyes.

Johnny is a man who don't want to be living so he
doesn't appear to be a man. All his life everyone
wanted him to be something. His Jewish mother
wanted him to be famous so he wouldn't live the life
she was living. The two main girlfriends he has had
wanted him to support them in the manner to which
they certainly weren't accustomed even though he
couldn't put his flabby hands on a penny. His father
wanted him to shut up.

All Johnny wants to do is make music. He wants
to keep everyone and everything who takes him
away from his music off him. Since he can't afford
human contact, he can't afford desire. Therefore he
hangs around with rich zombies who never have

anything to do with feelings. This is a typical New York artist attitude.

New York City is a pit-hole: Since the United States government, having decided that New York City is no longer part of the United States of America, is dumping all the laws the rich people want such as anti-rent-control laws and all the people they don't want (artists, poor minorities, and the media in general) on the city and refusing the city Federal funds; the American bourgeoisie has left. Only the poor: artists, Puerto Ricans who can't afford to move . . . and rich Europeans who fleeing the terrorists don't give a shit about New York . . . inhabit this city.

Meanwhile the temperature is getting hotter and hotter so no one can think clearly. No one perceives. No one cares. Insane madness come out like life is a terrific party.

In Front of the Mudd Club,
77 White Street

Two rich couples drop out of a limousine. The women are wearing outfits the poor people who were in ten years ago wore ten years ago. The men are just neutral. All the poor people who're making this club fashionable so the rich want to hang out here, even though the poor still never make a buck off the rich pleasure, are sitting on cars, watching the rich people walk up to the club.

Some creeps around the club's entrance. An open-shirted skinny guy who says he's just an artist is choosing who he'll let into the club. Since it's 3:30 A.M. there aren't many creeps. The artist won't let the rich hippies into the club.

— Look at that car.

– Jesus. It's those rich hippies' car.
– Let's take it.
– That's the chauffeur over there.
– Let's kidnap him.
– Let's knock him over the head with a bottle.
– I don't want no terrorism. I wanna go for a ride.
– That's right. We've got nothing to do with terr-
  orism. We'll just explain we want to borrow the
  car for an hour.
– Maybe he'll lend us the car if we explain we're
  terrorists-in-training. We want to use that car to
  try out terrorist tricks.

After 45 minutes the rich people climb back into their limousine and their chauffeur drives them away.

A girl who has gobs of brown hair like the foam on a cappuccino in Little Italy, black patent leather S&M heels, two unfashionable tits stuffed into a pale green corset, and extremely fashionable black fake leather tights heaves her large self off a car top. She's holding an empty bottle.

Diego senses there's going to be trouble. He gets off his car top. Is walking slowly towards the girl.

The bottle keeps waving. Finally the girl finds

some courage heaves the bottle at the skinny entrance artist.

The girl and the artist battle it out up the street. Some of the people who are sitting on cars separate them. We see the girl throw herself back on a car top. Her tits are bouncing so hard she must want our attention and she's getting insecure, maybe violent, cause she isn't getting enough. Better give us a better show. She sticks her middle finger into the air as far as she can. She writhes around on the top of the car. Her movements are so spasmatic she must be nuts.

A yellow taxi cab is slowly making its way to the club. On one side of this taxi cab's the club entrance. The other side is the girl writ(h)ing away on the black car. Three girls who are pretending to be transvestites are lifting themselves out of the cab elegantly around the big girl's body. The first body is encased into a translucent white girdle. A series of diagonal panels leads directly to her cunt. The other two dresses are tight and white. They are wriggling their way toward the club. The big girl, whom the taxi driver refused to let in his cab, wriggling because she's been rejected but not wriggling as much, is bumping into them. They're tottering away from her because she has syphilis.

Now the big girl is unsuccessfully trying to climb through a private white car's window now she's running hips hooking even faster into an alleyway taxi whose driver is locking his doors and windows against her. She's offering him a blow-job. Now an ugly boy with a huge safety pin stuck through his upper lip, walking up and down the street, is shooting at us with his watergun.

The dyke sitting next to me is saying earlier in the evening she pulled at this safety pin.

It's four o'clock A.M. It's still too hot. Wet heat's squeezing this city. The air's mist. The liquid's that seeping out of human flesh pores is gonna harden into a smooth shiny shell so we're going to become reptiles.

No one wants to move anymore. No one wants to be in a body. Physical possessions can go to hell even in this night.

Johnny like all other New York inhabitants doesn't want anything to do with sex. He hates sex because the air's hot, because feelings are dull, and because humans are repulsive.

Like all the other New Yorker's he's telling females he's strictly gay and males all faggots ought to burn in hell and they are. He's doing this because when he was sixteen years old his parents who wanted him to die stuck him in the Merchant Marines and all the marines cause this is what they do raped his ass off with many doses of coke.

Baudelaire doesn't go directly toward self-satisfaction cause of the following mechanism: X wants Y and, for whatever reasons reasons, thinks it shouldn't want Y. X thinks it is BAD because it wants Y. What X wants is Y and to be GOOD.

Baudelaire does the following to solve this dilemna: He understands that some agency (his parents, society, his mistress, etc.) is saying that wanting Y is BAD. This agency is authority is right. The authority will punish him because he's BAD. The authority will punish him as much as possible, punish me punish me, more than is necessary till it has to be obvious to everyone that the punishment is unjust. Punishers are unjust. All authority right now stinks to high hell. Therefore there is no GOOD and BAD. X cannot be BAD.

It's necessary to go to as many extremes as possible.

As soon as Johnny sees Janey he wants to have sex with her. Johnny takes out his cock and rubs it. He walks over to Janey, puts his arms around her shoulders so he's pinning her against a concrete wall.

Johnny says, "You're always talking about sex. Are

you going to spread your legs for me like you spread your legs all the time for any guy you don't know?"

Janey replies, "I'm not fucking anymore cause sex is a prison. It's become a support of this post-capitalist system like art. Businessmen who want to make money have to turn up a product that people'll buy and want to keep buying. Since American consumers now own every object there is plus they don't have any money anyway cause they're being squeezed between inflation and depression, just like fucking, these businessmen have to discover products that obvious necessity sells. Sex is such a product. Just get rid of the puritanism sweetheart your parents spoonfed you in between materialism which the sexual revolution did thanks to free love and hippies sex is a terrific hook. Sexual desire is a naturally fluctuating phenomena. The sex product presents a naturally expanding market. Now capitalists are doing everything they can to bring world sexual desire to an unbearable edge.

"I don't want to be hurt again. Getting hurt or rejected is more dangerous than I know because now everytime I get sexually rejected I get dangerously physically sick. I don't want to hurt again. Every time I hurt I feel so disgusted with myself – that by following some stupid body desire I didn't HAVE to follow, I killed the tender nerves of someone else. I retreat into myself. I again become frigid."

"I never have fun."

Johnny says, "You want to be as desperate as possible but you don't have to be desperate. You're going to be a success. Everybody knows you're going to be a success. Wouldn't you like to give up this artistic life which you know isn't rewarding cause artists now have to turn their work/selves into marketable objects/fluctuating images/fashion have to competitively knife each other in the back because we're not people, can't treat each other like people, no feelings, loneliness comes from the world of rationality, robots, every thing one as objects defined separate from each other? The whole impetus for art in the first place is gone bye-bye? You know you want to get away from this media world."

Janey replies, "I don't know what I want now. I know the New York City world is more complex and desirable even though everything you're saying's

true. I don't know what my heart is cause I'm corrupted."

"Become pure again. Love. You have to will. You can do what you will. Then love'll enter your heart."

"I'm not capable of loving anyone. I'm a freak. Love's an obsession that only weird people have. I'm going to be a robot for the rest of my life. This is confusing to be a human being, but robotism is what's present."

"It's unnatural to be sexless. You eat alone and that's freaky."

"I am lonely out of my mind. I am miserable out of my mind. Open open what are you touching me. Touching me. Now I'm going into the state where desire comes out like a monster. Sex I love you. I'll do anything to touch you. I've got to fuck. Don't you understand don't you have needs as much as I have needs DON'T YOU HAVE TO GET LAID?"

— Janey, close that door. What's the matter with
  you? Why aren't you doing what I tell you?
— I'll do whatever you tell me, nana.
— That's right. Now go into that drawer and get
  that checkbook for me. The Chase Manhattan
  one, not the other one. Give me both of them.
  I'll show you which one.
— I can find it, nana. No, it's not this one.
— Give me both of them. I'll do it.
— Here you are, nana. This is the one you want,
  isn't it?
— Now sit yourself down and write yourself out a
  check for $10,000. It doesn't matter which check
  you write it on.
— Ten thousand dollars! Are you sure about this,
  nana?
— Do what I tell you. Write yourself out a check for
  ten thousand dollars.
— Uh O.K. What's the date?
— It doesn't matter. Put any date you want. Now
  hand me my glasses. They're over there.
— I'm just going to clean them. They're dirty.

- You can clean them for me later. Give them to me.
- Are . . .you sure you want to do this?
- Now I'm going to tell you something, Janey. Invest this. Buy yourself 100 shares of AT&T. You can fritter it away if you want. Good riddance to you. If your mother had invested the 800 shares of IBM I gave her, she would have had a steady income and wouldn't have had to commit suicide. Well, she needed the money. If you invest in AT&T, you'll always have an income.
- I don't know what to say. I've never seen so much money before. I've never seen so much money before.
- You do what I tell you to. Buy AT&T.
- I'll put the money in a bank, nana, and as soon as it clears I'll buy AT&T.

At ten o'clock the next morning Nana is still asleep. A rich salesman who was spending his winter in New York had installed her in a huge apartment on Park Avenue for six months. The apartment's rooms are tremendous, too big for her tiny body, and are still partly unfurnished. Thick silk daybed spreads ivory-handled white feather fans hanging above contrast the black-and-red 'naturalistic' clown portraits in the 'study' that give an air of culture rather than of call-girl. A call-girl or mistress, as soon as her first man is gone, is no longer innocent. No one to help her, constantly harassed by rent and food bills, in need of elegant clothing and cosmetics to keep surviving, she has to use her sex to get money.

Nana's sleeping on her stomach, her bare arms hugging instead of a man a pillow into which she's buried a face soft with sleep. The bedroom and the small adjoining dressingroom are the only two properly furnished rooms. A ray of light filtered through the gray richly-laced curtain focuses a rosewood bedsteads covered by carved Chinese figures, the bedstead covered by white linen sheets; covered by a pale blue silk quilt; covered by a pale white silk quilt; Chinese pictures composed of five to seven layers of carved ivory, almost sculptures rather than pictures, surround these gleaming layers.

She feels around and, finding no one, calls her maid.

"Paul left ten minutes ago," the girl says as she walks into the room. "He didn't want to wake you. I asked him if he wanted coffee but he said he was in a rush. He'll see you his usual time tomorrow."

"Tomorrow tomorrow;" the prostitute can never get anything straight, "can he come tomorrow?"

"Wednesday's Paul's day. Today you see the furrier."

"I remember," she says, sitting up, "the old furrier told me he's coming Wednesday and I can't go against him. Paul'll have to come another day."

"You didn't tell me. If you don't tell me what's going on, I'm going to get things confused and your Johns'll be running into each other!"

Nana stretches her fatty arms over her head and yawns. Two bunches of short brown hairs are sticking out of her arm-pits. "I'll call Paul and tell him to come back tonight. No. I won't sleep with anyone tonight. Can I afford it? I'll tell Paul to come on Tuesdays after this and I'll have tonight to myself!" Her nightgown slips down her nipples surrounded by one long brown hair and the rest of her hair, loose and tousled, flows over her still-wet sheets.

Bet – I think feminism is the only thing that matters.

Janey – (yawning) – I'm so tired all I can do is sleep all day (only she doesn't fall asleep cause she's suddenly attracted to Michael who's like every other guy she's attracted to married to a friend of hers.)

Bet – First of all feminism is only possible in a socialist state.

Janey – But Russia stinks as much as the United States these days. What has this got to do with your film?

Bet – Cause feminism depends on four factors: First of all, women have to have economic independence. If they don't have that they don't have anything. Second, free daycare centers. Abortions. (counting on her fingers) Fourth, decent housing.

Janey – I mean those are just material considerations. You're accepting the materialism this society teaches. I mean look I've had lots of abortions I can fuck anyone I want – well, I could – I'm still in prison. I'm not talking about myself.

Bet – Are you against abortions?

Janey – How could I be against abortions? I've had fucking five of them. I can't be against abortions. I just think all that stuff is back in the 1920's. It doesn't apply to this world. This world is different than all that socialism: those multi-national corporations control everything.

Louie – You just don't know how things are cause the feminist movement here is nothing compared to the feminist movements in Italy, England, and Australia. That's where women really stick together.

Janey – That's not true! Feminism here, sure it's not the old feminism the groups Gloria Steinem and Ti-Grace, but they were *so* straight. It's much better now: it's just underground it's not so public.

Louie – The only women in Abercrombie's and Fitch's films are those traditionally male defined types.

The women are always whores or bitches. They have no power.

Janey – Women are whores now. I think women every time they fuck no matter who they fuck should get paid. When they fuck their boyfriends their husbands. That's the way things are only the women don't get paid.

Louie – Look at Carter's films. There are no women's roles. The only two women in the film who aren't bit players are France who's a bitch and England who's a whore.

Janey – But that's how things were in Rome of that time.

Bet – But, Jane, we're saying things have to be different. Our friends can't keep upholding the sexist state of women in their work.

Janey – You know about Abercrombie and Fitch. I don't even bother saying anything to them. But Carter's film: you've got to look at why an artist does what he does. Otherwise you're you're not being fair. In ROME Carter's saying the decadent Roman society was like this one.

Louie – The one that a certain small group of artists in New York lives in.

Janey – Yeah.

Louie – He's saying the men we know treat women only as whores and bitches.

Janey – So what are you complaining about?

Bet – Before you were saying you have no one to talk to about your work. That's what I'm saying. We've got to tell Abercrombie and Fitch what they're doing. We've got to start portraying women as strong showing women as the power of this society.

Janey – But we're not.

Bet – But how else are we going to be? In Italy there was this women's art festival. A friend of ours who does performance dressed as a woman and did a performance. Then he revealed he was a man. The women in the festival beat him up and called the police.

Michael – The police?

Janey – Was he good?

Bet – He was the best performer there.

Louie – I think calling the police is weird. They should have just beaten him up.

Janey – I don't like the police.

I Want All The Above To Be The Sun.

Intense Sexual Desire is the Greatest Thing in the World

Janey dreams of cocks. Janey sees cocks instead of objects.

Janey has to fuck.

This is the way Sex drives Janey crazy: Before Janey fucks, she keeps her wants in cells. As soon as Janey's fucking she wants to be adored as much as possible at the same time as, its other extreme, ignored as much as possible. More than this: Janey can no longer perceive herself wanting. Janey is Want.

It's worse than this: If Janey gets sexually rejected her body becomes sick. If she doesn't get who she wants she naturally revolts.

This is the nature of reality. No rationality possible. Only this is true. The world in which there is no

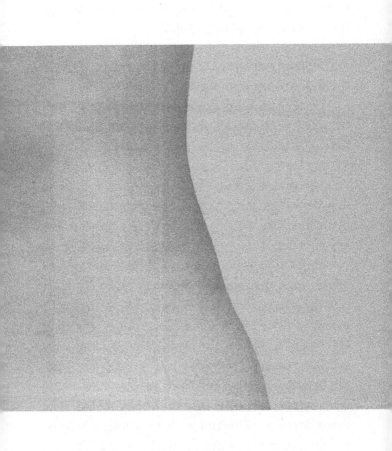

feeling, the robot world, doesn't exist. This world is a very dangerous place to live in.

Old women just cause they're old and no man'll fuck them don't stop wanting sex.

The old actress isn't good anymore. But she keeps on acting even though she knows all the audiences mock her hideousness and lack of context cause she adores acting. Her legs are grotesque: FLABBY. Above, hidden within the folds of skin, there's an ugly cunt. Two long flaps of white thin spreckled by black hairs like a pig's cock flesh hang down to the knees. There's no feeling in them. Between these two flaps of skin the meat is red folds and drips a white slime that poisons whatever it touches. Just one drop burns a hole into anything. An odor of garbage infested by maggots floats out of this cunt. One wants to vomit. The meat is so red it looks like someone hacked a body to bits with a cleaver or like the bright red lines under the purple lines on the translucent skin of a woman's body found dead three days ago. This red leads to a hole, a hole of redness, round and round, black nausea. The old actress is black nausea because she reminds us of death. Yet she keeps plying her trade and that makes her trade weird. Glory be to those humans who are absolutely NOTHING for the opinions of other humans: they are the true owners of illusions, transformations, and themselves.

Old people are supposed to be smarter than young people.

Old people in this country the United States of America are treated like total shit. Since most people spend their lives mentally dwelling on the material, they have no mental freedom, when they grow old and their skin rots and their bodies turn to putrefying sand and they can't do physical exercise and they can't indulge in bodily pleasure and they're all ugly anyway; suddenly they got nothing. Having nothing, you think they could at least be shut up in opiated dens so maybe they have a chance to develop dreams or at least they could warn their kids to do something else besides being materialistic. But the way this country's set up, there's not even opiated homes to hide this feelinglessness: old people have to go either to children's or most often into rest homes where they're shunted into wheelchairs and made as fast as possible into zombies cause it's easier to handle a zombie, if you have to handle anything, than a human. So an old person has a big empty hollow space with nothing in it, just ugh, and that's life: nothing else is going to happen, there's just ugh stop.

ANYTHING THAT DESTROYS LIMITS

Afterwards Janey and Johnny went to an all-night movie. All during the first movie Janey's sort of leaning against Johnny cause she's unsure he's attracted to her and she doesn't want to embarass him (her) in case he ain't. She kinda scrunches against him. One point Johnny is pressing his knee against her knee but she still ain't sure.

Some Like It Hot ends. All the rest of the painters are gonna leave the movie house cause they've seen *The Misfits*. Separately Janey and Johnny say they're going to stay. The painters are walking out. The movie theatre is black.

Janey still doesn't know what Johnny's feelings are.

A third way through the second movie Johnny's hand grabs her knee. Her whole body becomes crazy. She puts her right hand into his hand but he doesn't want the hand.

Johnny's hand, rubbing her tan leg, is inching closer to her cunt. The hand is moving roughly, grabbing handfuls of flesh, the flesh and blood crawling. He's not responding to anything she's doing.

Finally she's tentatively touching his leg. His hand is pouncing on her right hand setting it an inch below his cock. Her body's becoming even crazier and she's more content.

His other hand is inching slower toward her open slimy hole. Cause the theatre is small, not very dark, and the seats aren't too steep, everyone sitting around them is watching exactly what they're doing: Her black dress is shoved up around her young thighs. His hand is almost curving around her dark-pantied cunt. Her and his legs are intertwined. Despite fear she's sure to be arrested just like in a porn book because fear she's wanting him to stick his cock up her right now.

His hand is roughly travelling around her cunt, never touching nothing, smaller and smaller circles.

Morning. The movie house lights go on. Johnny looks at Janey like she's a business acquaintance. From now on everything Janey does is for the purpose of getting Johnny's dick into her:

Johnny, "Let's get out of here."

New York City at six in the morning is beautiful. Empty streets except for a few bums. No garbage. A slight shudder of air down the long long streets. Pale gray prevails. Janey's going to kill Johnny if he

doesn't give her his cock instantaneously. She's think-
ing ways to get him to give her his cock. Her body
becomes even crazier. Her body takes over. Turn on
him. Throw arms around his neck. Back him against
car. Shove clothed cunt against clothed cock. Lick ear
because that's what there is.

Lick your ear.

Lick your ear.

Well?

I don't know.

What don't you know? You don't know if you
want to?

Turn on him. Throw arms around his neck. Back
him against car. Shove clothed cunt against clothed
cock. Lick ear because that's what there is.

Obviously I want to.

I don't care what you do. You can come home
with me; you can take a rain check; you cannot take
a rain check.

I have to see my lawyer tomorrow. Then I have
lunch with Ray.

Turn on him. Throw arms around his neck. Back
him against car. Shove clothed cunt against clothed

cock. Lick ear because that's what there is.

You're not helping me much.

You're not helping me much.

Through this morning they walk to her apartment. Johnny and Janey don't touch. Johnny and Janey don't talk to each other.

Johnny is saying that Janey's going to invite him up for a few minutes.

Janey is pouring Johnny a glass of Scotch. Janey is sitting in her bedroom on her bed. Johnny is untying the string holding up her black sheath. Johnny's saliva-wettened fingers are pinching her nipple. Johnny is lifting her body over his prostrate body. Johnny's making her cunt rub very roughly through the clothes against his huge cock. Johnny's taking her off him and lifting her dress over her body. Janey's saying, "Your cock is huge." Janey's placing her lips around Johnny's huge cock. Janey's easing her black underpants over her feet.

Johnny's moaning like he's about to come. Janey's lips are letting go his cock. Johnny's lifting Janey's body over his body so the top of his cock is just touching her lips. His hands on her thighs are pulling her down fast and hard. His cock is so huge it is entering her cunt painfully. His body is immediately moving quickly violently shudders. The cock is entering the bottom of Janey's cunt. Janey is coming. Johnny's hands are not holding Janey's thighs firmly enough and Johnny's moving too quickly to keep Janey coming. Johnny is building up to coming.

That's all right yes I that's all right. I'm coming again smooth of you oh oh smooth, goes on and on, am I coming am I not coming.

Janey's rolling off of Johnny. Johnny's pulling the black pants he's still wearing over his thighs because he has to go home. Janey's telling him she has to sleep alone even though she isn't knowing what she's feeling. At the door to Janey's apartment Johnny's telling Janey he's going to call her. Johnny walks out the door and doesn't see Janey again.

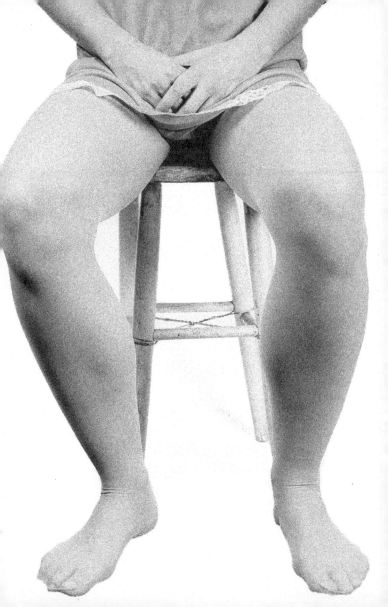